SISTERS

TRICIA TUSA

CROWN PUBLISHERS, INC.   New York

Published by Crown Publishers, Inc.,
a Random House company,
201 East 50th Street, New York, NY 10022

CROWN is a trademark of Crown Publishers, Inc.
Manufactured in Singapore
Library of Congress Cataloging-in-Publication Data
Tusa, Tricia
Sisters / written and illustrated by Tricia Tusa
        p.   cm.
Summary: Two sisters have an argument about how to cook
an artichoke, but they cannot stay mad at each other for
long—especially when the artichoke keeps turning up in the
most surprising places.
[1. Sisters—Fiction. 2. Quarreling—Fiction. 3. Artichokes—
Fiction.] I. Title.
PZ7.T8825Si   1995
[E]—dc20
94-39047

ISBN 0-517-70032-8 (trade)
      0-517-70033-6 (lib. bdg.)

10 9 8 7 6 5 4 3 2 1
First Edition

Lucy and Eeda had an argument

about an artichoke.

Lucy thought it should be boiled.
Eeda wanted it baked.

It turned out hard
and was impossible
to eat.

Lucy blamed Eeda.

Eeda blamed Lucy.

Both sisters went to bed mad,

without uttering a word.

A week passed and the silence continued.

Eeda went off for her wash and set.

While searching for a piece of Juicy Fruit gum,

she discovered something else in her purse.

That afternoon, Lucy received a package.

"For me? What could it be? Maybe it's the hat I ordered, or the fishing rod. Maybe it's the set of encyclopedias, *P* through *Z*."

The following morning, Eeda was unable
to decide between pancakes and corn flakes.

She settled for oatmeal.

Later that day,

Lucy relaxed in a hot tub.

It was Eeda's turn to fix supper.

Instead of her turkey meatloaf, she discovered
something else in the oven.

Simmering in garlic lemon butter,
the artichoke was stuffed with
crabmeat and covered in
bread crumbs, garnished with
a sprig of fresh parsley.

Eeda's favorite dish!

Quickly, she set
to work making
Lucy's favorite dessert.

The sisters applauded
one another's culinary skills.

"And wouldn't it be fun . . . ," said Lucy,
"to rearrange the den together?"

Lucy thought the armchair
would look nice *here*.

Eeda thought it would look nicer . . . *there*.

The next morning, Lucy went
to the refrigerator for the
pitcher of orange juice.